Malia Shaw is an eight-year-old from Pearland, Texas. She is currently in the 3rd grade and enjoys playing with her sister, dancing, boxing, tennis, and writing. Malia has always been a girl that loves to make up songs and write stories. When she grows up, she wants to be a tennis player and a doctor that delivers babies.

MALIA
THE
MAGNIFICENT!

Malia Shaw

Skit Skot

Zip Zap

Fro Frum

Flim Flam

Twirl Twirl

AUSTIN MACAULEY PUBLISHERS™

LONDON * CAMBRIDGE * NEW YORK * SHARJAH

Copyright © Malia Shaw (2020)

Ordering Information:
Quantity sales: special discounts are available on quantity purchases by corporations, associations, and others. For details, contact the publisher at the address below.

Publisher's Cataloging-in-Publication data
Shaw, Malia
Malia the Magnificent!

ISBN 9781647501365 (Paperback)
ISBN 9781647501358 (Hardback)
ISBN 9781647501372 (ePub e-book)

Library of Congress Control Number: 2019921279

www.austinmacauley.com/us

First Published (2020)
Austin Macauley Publishers LLC
40 Wall Street, 28th Floor
New York, NY 10005
USA

mail-usa@austinmacauley.com
+1 (646) 5125767

To my family and friends, I love you!

And to my parents, who allow me to explore everything my heart desires, thank you.

On show-and-tell day, Malia couldn't stop moving in her seat.

Because although some kids brought stuffed animals, night-lights, and action-figures to school, Malia knew that she brought the coolest thing of all!

When it was finally her turn, Malia quickly walked to the front of the class. Then she held up a notebook for everyone to see.

"This is no ordinary book," Malia said. "This is a SPELL BOOK! It is filled with magical spells that make wonderful things happen! Now, I would read you one of my spells today, but they are all top secret! I am going to use them when I start my traveling magic show!"

That day during recess, Malia's friends Jaelyn and London had a few questions for her.

"Malia, are you sure you want to be a magician?" Jaelyn asked.

"Yeah, being a magician when you grow up is gonna be really hard," said London. "You guys! I'm ALREADY a magician!" Malia proclaimed. "You are?" said London.

"Yeah! I've already used my spell book to make things happen! The spells don't always work the way I think they would, but that doesn't really matter."

I saw this really cool pair of light-up shoes in the shoe store one day,"
Malia said. "When I got home, I performed this spell—"

"Wait, aren't your spells top secret?" Jaelyn asked.

"Oh, Right! Well, I guess it's okay if I say them since you are my friends. So the spell was: Zip-Zap! Zip-Zap! Twirl-Twirl around! And touch the ground! Look at the cool new shoes I've found!"

"Did the shoes appear?" London asked.

"No, not that day," Malia said.

"But on my birthday, I opened up this pretty present and guess what was inside? The light-up shoes!"

"Another time I tried to pull a rabbit out of a hat. So I said: 'Skit-Skot! Skit-Skot Skat! Make a bunny come out of my hat!'"

"Did you pull a rabbit out of your hat?" Jaelyn asked.
"No, but when I went outside to get the mail, what did I see?"
"A little brown baby bunny!"

"I also used a spell to get a cat down from a tree! I said: 'Flim-Flam! Fro-Frum! Fee! Make this cat come down from the tree!'"

"Did the cat come down?" asked London. "Well, not right away, but a few hours after I said the spell, a fire truck came by and got the cat down!"

"I also turned my white shirt red one day because I wanted it to match my bow! I said: 'Swirl! Whirl! Tolly! Ted!'"

"It's time to turn my white shirt red!"

"Did your shirt turn red?" Jaelyn asked. "Not all of it!" Malia said.
"But then I was eating lunch that day I got some ketchup on my shirt.
And what color is ketchup?"

IT'S RED!

"I also made an apple disappear by saying: Hip-Hip Hurray! Now dance and cheer! This apple is going to disappear!"

"Did the apple disappear?" asked London.
"Well, when I came back outside the next day, something had eaten the apple, and I count that as disappearing."

"Wow... I guess you really can do magic." Jaelyn said.
"That's right! I'm Malia the Magnificent! And I can do anything
I set my mind to!"

CPSIA information can be obtained
at www.ICGtesting.com
Printed in the USA
LVHW072130130121
676435LV00045B/1442

9 781647 501365